Little Skink's Tail

By Janet Halfmann   Illustrated by Laurie Allen Klein

With love to my granddaughter Monae, a bundle of inspiration—JH
To Bob & Jesse—LAK
Thanks to Sherry Crawley, Director of Education, School and Family Programs at Zoo Atlanta for verifying the accuracy of the information in this book.

Publisher's Cataloging-In-Publication Data

Halfmann, Janet.

Little Skink's tail / by Janet Halfmann ; illustrated by Laurie Allen Klein.

p. : col. ill. ; cm.

Summary: While Little Skink hunts for breakfast, she is attacked by a crow and escapes by snapping off her tail. Little Skink's Tail follows her as she daydreams of having the tails of other animals in the forest. Includes "For Creative Minds" section with information on tail adaptations, matching activity, and a footprint map activity.
ISBN: 978-0-97688-238-1 English hardcover
ISBN: 978-1-60718-864-3 English pbk.
ISBN: 978-1-62855-374-1 Spanish pbk.
ISNB: 978-1-60718-0227 English eBook downloadable
ISBN: 9781934359570 Spanish eBook downloadable
Interactive, read-aloud eBook featuring selectable English (978-1-60718-2689) and Spanish (978-1-62855-099-3) text and audio (web and iPad/tablet based)
1. Skinks--Juvenile fiction. 2. Tail--Juvenile fiction. 3. Skinks--Fiction. 4. Tail--Fiction.
I. Klein, Laurie Allen. II. Title.
PZ10.3.H136 Li 2007[E]   2007920038

Manufactured in the USA
This product conforms to CPSIA 2008

Arbordale Publishing
formerly Sylvan Dell Publishing
Mt. Pleasant, SC 29464
www.ArbordalePublishing.com

04 16

Little Skink basked on a big yellow rock in the rays of the morning sun. Her chilly body soon turned snugly warm. She twitched her bright blue tail.

The little lizard was ready to start her day.

Leaping to the forest floor,
she poked her pointy nose
into a crack in a rotting log
and looked for breakfast.
Sniff, sniff! She smelled ants.

She loved ants!

Gobble, gobble, gobble.
She gulped down one ant
after another.

Her tummy was almost full
when she felt a peck on her tail.
It was a large, hungry crow!

Little Skink was trapped. There was no way to run. But she had a trick . . .

Quicker than the crow could blink, Little Skink snapped off her bright blue tail!

Wiggle, waggle, wiggle, went the tail, wriggling wildly through the fallen leaves.

The crow forgot all about Little Skink. It wanted that wiggling, waggling tail!

As the crow bounced this way and that, Little Skink slinked under a log. She was safe.

Her wiggling, waggling tail had saved her.

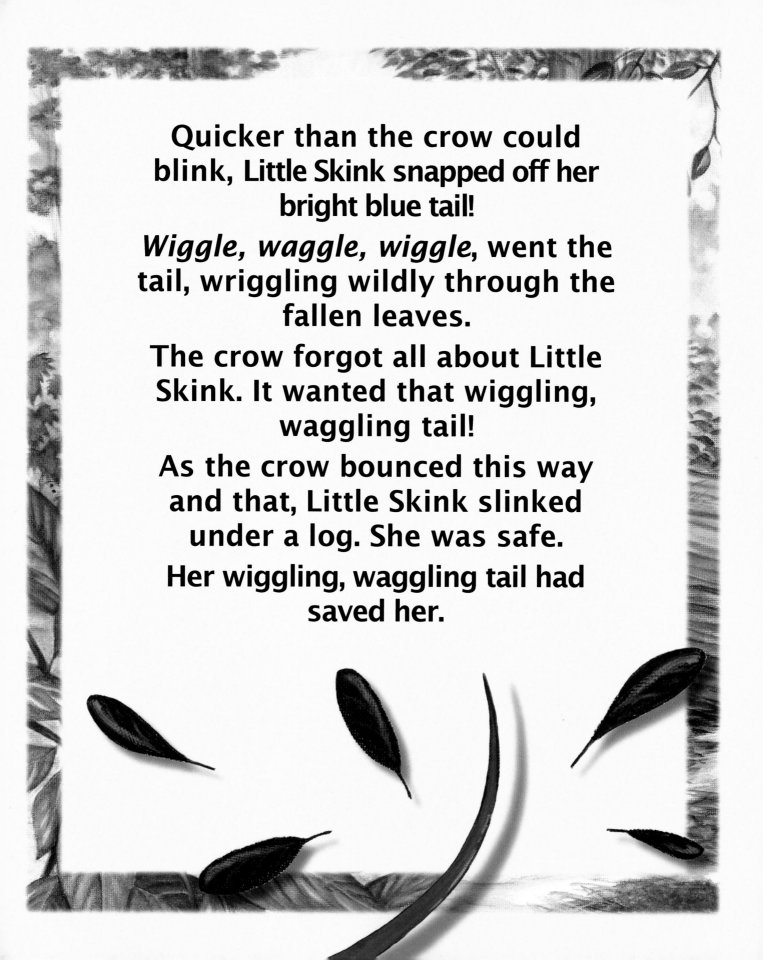

The next morning, as Little Skink basked on her rock, she felt a little sad.

She missed her bright blue tail, even though she was happy to be alive.

As she lay basking and thinking, a cottontail rabbit hopped in front of her rock.

Hmmm, I wonder how I'd look with a tail like that?" Little Skink thought.

She pictured her new look. "Very cute," she thought to herself, "but too *puffy-fluffy*."

Next, she tried a squirrel's tail: "It's fun to flick and fluff," she said, "but much too bushy."

Day after day, Little Skink imagined herself wearing the tail of every animal she met.

A deer's tail: "Look! I can wave it like a little flag," she said. "But it's so short and stubby."

A skunk's tail: "Peeeuuw!" said Little Skink. "*Stinky, stinky, stinky!*"

A porcupine's tail: "Too *stickly-prickly*," she said.

An owl's tail: "A lizard with feathers?" she exclaimed.

"I don't think so!"

A turtle's tail: "Too pointy," said Little Skink.

While all were fine tails, not one was quite right for her.

Then one day as she scampered onto her sunny rock, her shadow caught her eye . . .

Her shadow had a tail!

She whipped around. Sure enough, her tail had grown back.

"A skink needs a skink's tail," she said, and her tail-dreaming days were over.

For Creative Minds

Footprint Map

Using the animal footprints as hints, can you identify where Little Skink saw the animals in the woods? Find the number and the letter of the box that identifies the animal tracks. For example, Little Skink is located in box 7, D.

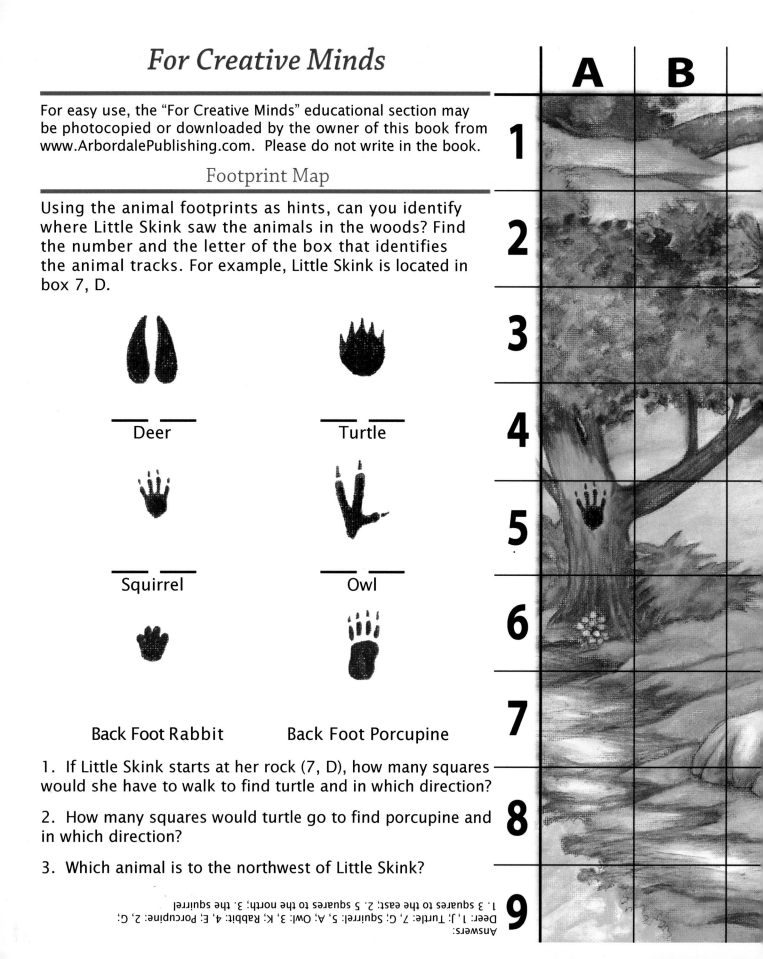

Deer

Turtle

Squirrel

Owl

Back Foot Rabbit

Back Foot Porcupine

1. If Little Skink starts at her rock (7, D), how many squares would she have to walk to find turtle and in which direction?

2. How many squares would turtle go to find porcupine and in which direction?

3. Which animal is to the northwest of Little Skink?

A B

1 2 3 4 5 6 7 8 9

Answers:
Deer: 1, J; Turtle: 7, G; Squirrel: 5, A; Owl: 3, K; Rabbit: 4, E; Porcupine: 2, G; 1. 3 squares to the east; 2. 5 squares to the north; 3. the squirrel

Why Do Animals Have Tails? A Tail Matching Activity

Animals use tails in many different ways: to protect themselves, to balance or steer, to talk to other animals, or to attract other animals to them (either a mate or prey). Some animals can even store food in their tails or can use tails like a hand to hold onto things (prehensile). *Can you match the animal to its tail?*

1.

2.

3.

4.

5.

6.

7.

a. Skink
Little Skink's tail came off but kept wriggling in order to confuse the crow. That gave Little Skink a chance to get away: she used her tail to protect herself.

b. Cottontail Rabbit
A cottontail rabbit's tail is dark on top and light on the bottom. A rabbit raises its tail when trying to tell other cottontails that there is trouble.

c. Squirrel
A squirrel uses its tail to balance as it runs and jumps from one tree branch to another.

d. White-Tailed Deer
A white-tailed deer raises its tail to warn other deer of danger.

e. Skunk
If scared, a skunk will protect itself by raising its tail to release a stinky spray.

f. Porcupine
A porcupine will rub its tail against an animal and release quills into the animal.

g. Owl
An owl uses its tail to help balance and steer as it flies.

Answers:
1. b; 2. f; 3. c; 4. g; 5. a; 6. d; 7. e